THE GIRL WHO
Shared Kindness

WRITTEN BY TAYLOR KOELBL AND DANIELLE DEPRATT KOELBL

ILLUSTRATED BY ERIN BONHAM

Notes from the Author

Taylor and I wrote this book after a conversation about a friend who felt left out in class because she was the only child that celebrated a specific holiday. After we wrote this story, I asked Taylor if the things that make children sad in the story were based upon her friends. Her response broke my heart," No mommy. Those were all about me."

Please enjoy our heartfelt story. If we lift each other up and share a little kindness, perhaps each person will feel a little warmer inside.

-Danielle Depratt Koelbl

SUPPORT AUTHOR ALEX KOELBL

EDITED BY LAURA JOECKEL AND JENNIFER MAGGENTI

There once was a girl who saw
her friend sitting with a sad face.

"What's wrong?" asked the girl.

"I'm sad because I don't like my
curly hair," the friend replied.

The girl was surprised.

"Really? Your curly locks bounce along happily

when you walk." The girl continued,

"And...I like being your friend because you are

nice to me and make me smile.

Thank you for being you."

The friend's eyes sparkled as she fluffed her curly hair, stood up tall, and smiled proudly. The friends joined hands and went outside to play.

The next day the girl's friend saw a boy

sitting with a sad face.

"What's wrong?" asked the friend.

The boy responded, "I'm sad because I do

not run as fast as the other kids."

"Well, you sure hit a baseball hard because you made it all the way to second base the other day! Even if you are not the fastest runner, I like being your friend because you go on exploring adventures with me."

The boy smiled proudly as he stretched his legs long and stood up tall. The friends joined hands and went outside to play.

The next day the boy saw a classmate

sitting with a sad face.

"What's wrong?" asked the boy.

"I feel alone because no one in our class

celebrates the same holidays as me,"

said the girl.

"I loved when you told us about your holidays because I learned something new."

The boy continued, "And I like being your friend because you like to color and paint pictures just like me."

The girl stood up tall and smiled proudly.

The friends joined hands

and went outside to play.

The next day the girl saw a boy

sitting with a sad face.

"What's wrong?" asked the girl.

The boy responded, "I'm not allowed to

use a tablet or phone. I feel left out

because I don't know about the shows and

characters other kids talk about."

"I'm not allowed to use a tablet or phone either!" exclaimed the girl. "I have an idea. Let's make up a show and characters together. We can share our ideas with our friends and maybe they will join us!"

The boy stood up tall and smiled proudly

as new ideas swirled around in his head.

The friends joined hands and went

outside to play.

The next day there were no kids

sitting with a sad face.

Instead there were…

...five friends smiling and

standing proudly together.

Each girl and boy felt good inside because

each had given kindness to another.

Message in Motion

1. Name two of your friends.

2. What are two things you enjoy about each friend?

3. Next time you see each friend, share the two things you like about them.

Discover more from **The Girl Who stories collection**

The Girl Who Loves Unicorns
Just Believe. A sweet and suspenseful story about a young child's ongoing determination to find a unicorn. The girl tries and fails, repeatedly, but does not quit. In the end, will the girl find a unicorn through use of love, support and creativity. Or will she continue to have faith and believe in something she has never seen but knows is out there in theory, imagination or actuality.

The Girl Who Asked for Presents
A story about a young child who is constantly asking for new things. The child's clever parents decide to wrap common objects as gifts, which guides the child towards exploring her own unique creativity and discover new ways to play with old toys. Young children quickly identify with and enjoy the moral this story provides. Find beauty in an empty box. Find beauty within you.

Made in United States
North Haven, CT
15 November 2021